Horatio Solves a Mystery

Eleanor Clymer

Horatio Solves a Mystery

ILLUSTRATED BY

Robert Quackenbush

ATHENEUM *1980* NEW YORK

LIBRARY OF CONGRESS CATALOGING IN PUBLICATION DATA

Library of Congress Cataloging in Publication Data

Clymer, Eleanor Lowenton, date—
Horatio solves a mystery.

SUMMARY: *Horatio is not concerned about the missing*
items around the house until it is his catnip tiger
that is missing. Then he goes on the prowl
for the culprit.
[1. Cats—Fiction. 2. Monkeys—Fiction]
I. Quackenbush, Robert M. II. Title.
PZ7.C6272Hl   [E]   79-22590
ISBN 0-689-30734-9

For Roderick, Douglas and Ian   E.C.
and for Piet and Hansy   R.Q.

HORATIO lay in his favorite chair, curled up like a doughnut. Mrs. Casey sat in her chair, knitting. The clock ticked, the knitting needles clicked. It was a warm night. Through the open windows came the sounds of people walking in the street. From the house next door came bumps and thumps. Some new people had moved in and were moving their furniture around.

"I must go and call on them soon," said Mrs. Casey. "Not this evening, though." And she went on knitting.

Everything was peaceful.

Horatio and Mrs. Casey were alone together. Goldilocks, the lady cat who lived with them, was away in the country with her two kittens. Mrs. Casey had nobody but Horatio to take care of. He liked it that way

Mrs. Casey was knitting a sweater for one of her grandchildren.

"I wonder if this is long enough," she said, reaching for her tape measure.

At that moment a little bell in the kitchen went "Ping!"

"My cake is done," said Mrs. Casey.

She took off her glasses, which she used for reading and knitting. She put down the sweater and the tape measure and went to take the cake out of the oven.

Horatio went, too. It was a good time to re-mind her that he had not had his evening snack of kitty-crackers and milk.

He sat in front of the refrigerator to show her where the milk was kept.

Mrs. Casey took the cake out of the oven, tested it with a toothpick, and put it on a rack to cool. Then she poured Horatio's milk.

When they returned to the living room, Mrs. Casey took up her knitting again and looked for the tape measure. But it was not there.

"Horatio, have you been playing with my tape measure?" she asked.

It was the kind that curled up into a little round case. When Horatio was young, he had enjoyed knocking it around the floor. But he had not done such a silly thing in years. He was a dignified middle-aged cat and did not play childish games.

He sat down to wash his face. He was not interested in tape measures.

Mrs. Casey emptied her knitting basket. She looked under her chair. She looked under the cushions of the chair.

Horatio wished she would sit down and stop fussing. But Mrs. Casey was unhappy.

"I just can't stand it when something is missing," she said. "Maybe I left it in the kitchen."

She went to look, but it was not there. She came back and searched all over the living room.

"Horatio, where is my tape measure?" she demanded.

Horatio was getting tired of this. He got up and yawned, stretched, and went upstairs to bed.

After a while Mrs. Casey came, too. Horatio hoped she had forgotten the tape measure.

But she hadn't. The next day she looked for it again.

"A tape measure does not just disappear," she said. "Horatio, you must have been playing with it."

She looked under his cushion, in his chair, and in the basket where he sometimes took a nap. She looked under her bed, and in fact, all over the house.

"Now, Horatio," she said, "there has not been anybody here but you and me, and I know *I* didn't lose that tape measure."

That afternoon Michael and Betsy were coming to tea. They were two children who lived nearby.

Horatio liked them. Long ago, when they were much younger, they used to bother him by rubbing his fur the wrong way or using him for a sofa cushion. But now they were bigger and had more sense. They just scratched him under the chin and gave him a piece of cat candy. Then they let him alone.

Mrs. Casey had baked the cake the night before just for them.

"I'll go and frost it right now," she said. "Fudge frosting, that's their favorite kind."

But when she went into the kitchen, what a sight met her eyes! The beautiful cake had a big chunk torn out of it.

"Horatio!" she called. "Come here this minute!"

Horatio didn't like the sound of her voice. He was not used to being spoken to like that.

Taking his time, he strolled slowly into the kitchen.

"Look at that cake!" she scolded. "Did you do that?"

Horatio might have rubbed against her ankles to show her that he felt sorry about it.

But since she was so cross, he just sat down and scratched his ear. After all, she ought to know he didn't eat cake.

Mrs. Casey cut off the torn piece and frosted the cake as well as she could.

Soon Michael and Betsy arrived. They had been away, visiting their grandmother in California. They brought Mrs. Casey a beautiful new case for her glasses.

"Oh, thank you," she said, and put her glasses in it. "It's just what I need. I'm always taking them off and putting them on again."

For Horatio, they brought a lovely present. It was a catnip tiger.

Horatio had a catnip mouse and a plain bag of catnip, rather grubby. But he had never had a catnip tiger. The outside was striped black and orange, and it had a long tail. It smelled delicious.

Horatio grabbed it, bit it, licked it, held it in all four feet, and lay on his back. Then he turned a somersault, threw it up in the air, caught it, and leaped around the room.

"He certainly likes that tiger," said Michael.

"I was the one who picked it out," said Betsy.

Horatio put the tiger in his chair and sat on it, to make sure nobody took it away from him.

"Now let's go and have our cake," said Mrs. Casey. "I made a chocolate cake with fudge frosting just for you."

"Mmmm! Good!" said Michael and Betsy.

They went into the dining room and Mrs. Casey brought in the cake.

"It had an accident," she said, cutting slices and scooping out ice cream. "Somebody broke off a piece."

"Who could have done that?" Michael asked.

"There was nobody here but Horatio and me," said Mrs. Casey, "and I'm sure I didn't do it."

"It doesn't sound like Horatio," said Betsy.

They went back to the living room. Horatio was sound asleep with his chin on his tiger.

"We have to go now," said Michael. "Mother told us to come home early."

"Thank you for the eyeglass case," said Mrs. Casey. "Let me see, didn't I put it on the table? It's gone."

"Gone!" exclaimed the children. "That's impossible!"

They looked all over the floor, in the chairs, on the sofa, on the mantel shelf, in the dining room. But the eyeglasses in their new case were not to be found.

"There must be elves around here," said Betsy.

"Or spacemen," said Michael.

"Or Horatio?" suggested Mrs. Casey.

"Did you take them to the kitchen?" Michael asked. "Are they in your knitting basket?"

No. They weren't anywhere.

Horatio woke up. They were bothering him. Why didn't they sit down and keep quiet?

"Maybe you took them upstairs," said Betsy.

Mrs. Casey couldn't remember going upstairs, but just to make sure they went up and looked all around.

They even leaned out of the window to see if the glasses were on the ground.

There was a tree in the yard. Betsy peered into its branches. "Maybe a bird flew in and took them to its nest," she said.

"Don't be silly," said Michael.

The children went home. Mrs. Casey stared at Horatio. She couldn't see to knit without her glasses, and it made her cross not to be able to find them.

When she gave Horatio his supper, she put the saucer down with a thump and walked away, not even waiting to see if he liked it. He rubbed against her ankles and said, "Meow!" But when she didn't answer he walked away.

He went to look for his catnip tiger. That would cheer him up.

But the tiger was gone!

Where could it be? Horatio looked in his chair, in his basket, in Mrs. Casey's chair. He sniffed in all the corners and under the sofa.

Somebody had taken his tiger. Who could have done it?

The kittens! But no, the kittens were in the country.

Horatio sat down and tried to think. Thinking wasn't easy. It was better to look. He went back to the kitchen.

Mrs. Casey was fixing her own supper. She put it on a tray and carried it to the dining room.

"Meow?" Horatio asked her.

She didn't answer. She just looked cross.

Suddenly he knew. Mrs. Casey must have taken his tiger and hidden it on purpose, just because she was angry. Well, now he was angry, too.

He trotted to the kitchen, jumped on the counter, and sniffed at the shelves. The only smells were kitchen ones like onions and soap.

He jumped down and knocked over the wastepaper basket. He began rummaging through the trash. Mrs. Casey heard him and came out to the kitchen.

"Horatio, you bad cat!" she exclaimed. "I don't know what's the matter with you today!"

Horatio scratched at the kitchen door.

"All right, go outside," she said, opening the door.

Horatio ran out. It was a warm summer evening. If it hadn't been for all this trouble, he would have been glad to be out. He might have met some other cats who lived nearby. But suddenly he thought, "Maybe Mrs. Casey threw my tiger out into the yard!" If one of those cats had found his tiger, he would never see it again.

He prowled in the yard, sniffing and scratching here and there. But there was no smell of catnip. He even climbed up into a rosebush, in case it had landed among the branches. The thorns pricked him, and he jumped down.

Grumpily he went back to the kitchen door. It was not locked. He gave it a push with his shoulder. It swung open and he walked in.

Mrs. Casey was sitting in her chair trying to read without her glasses and looking cross.

"May as well go up to bed," he thought. "Maybe by tomorrow she'll be feeling better."

Horatio walked into the hall and started up the stairs.

Suddenly he caught a whiff of something. Was it catnip? Yes, but very faint.

He went up the stairs. Ah! Now he was getting warmer. The smell was stronger now. He ran into Mrs. Casey's room. Here the smell was still stronger. In fact, little flakes of catnip were scattered on the floor.

Was there really something the matter with Mrs. Casey? Had she taken his tiger to play with? He couldn't believe it. It wasn't like her at all.

In the corner of the room was a tall closet. Horatio knew it well. He had once spent a whole day up there to get away from children and kittens. From the top of the closet, tiny flakes of catnip drifted down.

Horatio leaped to the bed in order to see better. On top of the closet something red was moving about.

It was a little creature with a long tail. It was wearing a red jacket and little pants. It had his tiger in its paws and was tearing it open and stuffing catnip into the pockets of its jacket. When it saw Horatio, it sat up and stared at him. Its eyes were round and bright.

Horatio was furious. Who was this creature, and what right did it have to tear open his new catnip tiger? He jumped to the closet. Then he hooked the red jacket in his claws and pulled.

The little animal squeaked and wriggled loose. Quick as a flash it jumped to Mrs. Casey's dressing table. It began to take the tops off the boxes there and throw them on the floor, chattering excitedly.

Horatio leaped to the floor, clutching the red jacket in his teeth. He ran down the stairs into the hall. Mrs. Casey looked up.

"What's that red thing you have there, Horatio?" she asked.

She got up and started toward him. But at that moment the doorbell rang. Mrs. Casey opened the door. There stood a woman. She started to talk excitedly. She had lost something, it seemed.

"I don't know where he went," she said.

Then she saw Horatio.

"Look!" she said. "The cat has got his jacket! Oh, my poor Jocko! I hope the cat hasn't hurt him!"

Mrs. Casey reached for the jacket. "Where did you get that?" she demanded. "Let me have it."

But Horatio would not give it to her. He wanted it. It was not as good as his tiger, but it did smell of catnip.

He ran back upstairs, and the two ladies rushed after him. Horatio ran into the bedroom and leaped to the closet. There he would be safe. In leaping, he knocked something down.

"My glasses!" Mrs. Casey exclaimed. "And my tape measure."

But the strange lady was not interested in those things.

"Jocko!" she cried. "You bad monkey!"

Powder was all over the floor. Mrs. Casey's jewelry box was open and the little creature with the long tail was tangled up in strings of beads. When he heard his name, he began to chatter.

"Come here, Jocko," said the lady, holding out her hand. In her fingers was a cooky. "Come on, Jocko," she coaxed.

The monkey leaped to her shoulder with a loud clatter of beads. While he munched the cooky, she snapped a collar around his neck and then took off the beads.

"I'm sorry about the mess," she said. "I'll get you some more powder."

"Oh, don't bother," said Mrs. Casey. "I'm so glad to have my glasses back. And I'm glad to meet my new neighbor. But how did Jocko get in here?"

"It was so warm, I left my windows open," said the lady. "And, you see, there's a tree between us. He must have jumped out of my window into the tree and from there to your window. Thank you for finding him."

"Don't thank me," said Mrs. Casey. "Thank Horatio. He's the one who found him."

"He's the smartest cat I ever saw," said the lady. "I must get him a present. Do you like catnip, Horatio?"

Horatio did not bother to answer such a foolish question. He stalked out of the room, carrying what was left of his tiger.

LATER, when everything had been tidied up, Mrs. Casey took Horatio on her lap.

"Poor Horatio," she said. "I'm so sorry. To think I blamed you! I should have known better."

"I couldn't agree more," said Horatio to himself.

Just then the door bell rang. Michael and Betsy dashed in.

"Oh, Mrs. Casey!" they cried. "Guess what! We just had to come and tell you. The new lady on the other side of you has a monkey! We just saw her with it."

Mrs. Casey smiled. "I know," she said. "I found out from Horatio."